You Will Always Be My Dad

Illustrations: Ann de Bode
Original title: *Maar jij blijft mijn papa*
© Van In, Lier, 1995. Van In Publishers, Grote Markt 39,
2500 Lier, Belgium.
© in this edition Evans Brothers Limited 1997
(world English rights excluding the USA and Canada)
English text by Su Swallow

First published in paperback in 1999

First published in Great Britain by
Evans Brothers Limited
2A Portman Mansions
Chiltern Street
London W1M 1LE

Printed by KHL (Singapore)

0 237 52045 1

HELPING HANDS

YOU WILL ALWAYS BE MY DAD

ANN DE BODE AND RIEN BROERE

Evans Brothers Limited

It's the school play. Everyone is laughing and
shouting and getting ready for the show.
All the mums and dads have been invited.
The children are dressing up in funny clothes
and painting their faces.
But Laura sits quietly at the table.
She doesn't want to join in.

'What's the matter?' asks Tim.
'Nothing,' says Laura. 'I just don't feel in the mood.'
Tim thinks something must be wrong.
Laura usually loves acting.
He puts his arm round her.
'Tell me what's wrong,' he says.
So Laura tells him why she is unhappy.
'Nobody's coming to see me,' she says, crying.

Laura's mum and dad don't live together now.
They didn't love each other enough any more.
Her dad moved to another house.
Laura and her brother Thomas go to stay with him
every two weeks, but it's not the same.
At first Laura thought: 'It's all my fault.'
But her mum said: 'You mustn't think that.
It's just a problem between Dad and me.'

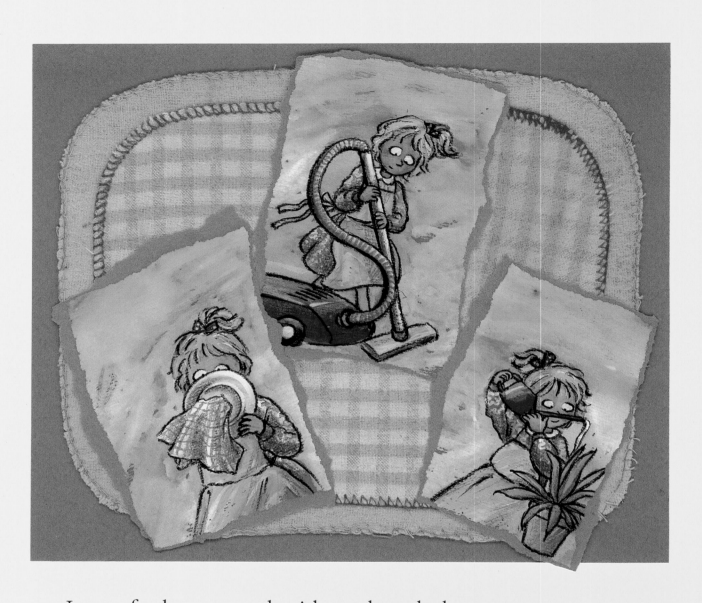

Laura feels very sad without her dad.
It's much worse than losing her favourite doll
or tearing her best trousers.
And she has to do more to help at home.
She washes up and hoovers and waters the plants.
It used to be Dad who did these jobs.
Deep down, Laura hopes he will come back,
because Mum and Dad belong together.

Laura's dad often makes a fuss of her
and gives her presents, as if to say 'sorry'.
Laura pretends to be pleased,
but what she really wants is for
everything to be the way it used to be.
Mum, Dad, Thomas and her, all together again.
But that's a present she can't have.

Laura gets ready for the show after all.
Tim has managed to cheer her up.
He knows just how she feels.
His parents are separated too.
'At least yours didn't argue all the time,' he says.
'Mine did. It was awful.
Sometimes they even threw things at each other.
I was quite glad when they separated.'

Now Tim doesn't look very happy.
'Why are you sad all of a sudden?' asks Laura.
'Oh, nothing,' says Tim, shrugging his shoulders.
'Are you thinking about your mum and dad?'
'Yes,' says Tim, sighing.
Laura understands how he feels.
She often thinks about her mum and dad,
and how it used to be.

Laura peeps through the curtains.
The hall is nearly full.
So many mums and dads!
Suddenly she jumps for joy.
There's Mum! She came after all.
Mum spots Laura and waves.
Laura is so excited she waves back with both hands,
as if she hadn't seen Mum for a week!

And look! Dad is there too!
He smiles and waves.
Laura knows where he can sit.
She points to an empty seat.
Dad moves along the row.
Just as he is about to sit down,
he realises who is next to him.
Brilliant, thinks Laura. I did well there!

Soon, it's Laura's turn on the stage.
She stands in the spotlight. She can't see into the hall
but she knows that Mum and Dad are there.
So she sings better than ever before.
She feels like a real star.
When the music stops, everyone claps loudly.
She bows, again and again.
She wants the clapping to go on for ever.

'What a good singer you are!' says Mum after the show.
'Where is Dad?' asks Laura.
'I don't know. I expect he's gone home.'
What a pity, thinks Laura. She had hoped...
'And what did you think of it?' asks Mum.
'It was all right,' says Laura.
'All right?' says Mum. 'But you were a star!
I was so proud of you, I couldn't sit still!'

Back home, Thomas goes straight to his room.
'Go and pack your case, Laura,' says Mum.
'Don't forget you're staying with Dad tomorrow.'
'What's the rush?' asks Laura.
'We're going to have a visitor - a man...
it's someone I like, and he likes me too.'
Laura suddenly feels very strange.
We don't need a man in our house, she thinks.

On her way upstairs Laura thinks about this visitor.
What will he be like?
She tries to picture him, but it's not easy.
Is he bald? Has he got big ears or a funny nose?
Perhaps he's very fat, or very old.
Laura imagines someone very ugly.
Then she thinks, no, if he was like that, Mum
wouldn't like him. So what is he like?

Laura decides to go and tell Thomas about the visitor.
But he doesn't seem very surprised.
'I knew already,' he says. 'It's good, isn't it?
Mum has got a friend again.
They'll be able to do lots of nice things together.'
'But what about Dad?' asks Laura.
'Dad will always be Dad,' says Thomas.
'That won't change.
Now off you go. I've got football training.'

For a while, Laura feels cross with
the whole world.
Then she begins to smile. And wrinkle her nose.
She has a plan. One that will spoil everything.
She will be very naughty, and nasty too.
She'll talk about Dad all the time.
Then let's see if this man still wants
to be Mum's friend.

Mum is rushing about all over the place,
tidying up and and moving things around.
'Take your feet off the table,' she grumbles.
'OK,' says Laura, and takes off her shoes.
Mum sees them on the table.
'What are they doing there?' she asks crossly.
'You only said to take my feet off the table.
So I did.'

'This man must be a king,' says Laura.
'Whatever do you mean?' asks Mum.
'Well, the table doesn't usually look this posh.'
Then, when Mum looks over at her,
Laura starts to pick her nose.
'Laura, stop being rude.'
'I'm not being rude. I'm doing it with
my little finger. That's polite, isn't it?'

Mum's visitor arrives.
'Laura, this is John. Come and say hello.'
'Hi,' says Laura, waving a hand at him.
She peers sideways at him.
Not bald, and no nasty spots.
He looks quite normal, and friendly.
But that doesn't make any difference, thinks Laura.
I've seen enough. Now get lost!

Mum has gone off to the kitchen.
Laura pulls an ugly face at John.
That'll do it, she thinks. Go away! Go away!
John starts to laugh, and he winks at her.
He doesn't seem to realise that Laura has
some nasty plans worked out.
Why does he keep gazing at me
like a sheep? Laura wonders.

John gets up. But not to go away.
He starts looking at the books in the bookcase.
'We used to have a lot more...' says Laura.
'Before, when...'
'When your dad was still at home,' says John.
'Yes, it's a shame, but it happens sometimes.'
Laura is confused. Is he talking about the books
or about Mum and Dad?

'The table looks very smart,' says John.
'Do you always eat like this?'
'Like what?' asks Laura.
'Well, it's like being in a restaurant.'
'Of course it's always like this,' replies Laura.
'And so it should be,' says John.
'It's what you would expect in the home
of a beautiful little princess.'

Laura slurps her soup.
'Eat properly,' Mum grumbles.
'OK,' says Laura, holding up
her little finger and sipping noisily.
'Laura!' Mum shouts.
That makes John jump and drop his spoon.
Soup splashes everywhere.
'Whoops,' he says. 'I'm sorry.'

John is sitting in Dad's place.
He shouldn't be there, thinks Laura.
But deep down, she likes him,
although she doesn't want to admit it.
She feels very confused.
Everything keeps going round and round
in her head. And it's all because
of the stupid separation, she thinks.

Ever since Mum and Dad split up,
everything is in a muddle.
Even her plot against John has gone wrong.
She wanted to do something very naughty.
Then he would have got angry and left.
But instead, he's still here.
When Laura gets up, she knocks a cup
on the floor. There, you see? Broken!

'Who would like some more?' asks Mum.
'Not for me, thank you,' says John. 'I'm full up.'
'Huh! Dad could eat six bowls of soup,' says Laura.
'And nine plates of meat and potato.
And four pies.
And an apple to finish.'
'Goodness me!' says John, very impressed.
But he doesn't move.

'I could never eat that much,' says John.
'But I can do this.'
He picks up a spoon
and rubs his finger over it.
He closes his hand, and opens it again.
No spoon! Now it's Laura's turn to be surprised.
'Oh! I can see it,' laughs John.
And he pulls out the spoon from behind Laura's ear.

I'll try once more, thinks Laura.
I'll scare him so much, he'll run away.
'My dad is very strong,' she says.
'When he's angry, he can smash that cupboard
into a thousand pieces, all in one go.
'Goodness!' says John again.
'But he's not often angry, is he?'
'How do you know?' asks Laura in surprise.
'Well,' says John. 'The cupboard is still there.'

Suddenly Laura leaps up. Only a few minutes
to go before Dad picks her up.
And he will see John. But he mustn't!
She runs off to her room.
'Is there a fire?' Mum asks in surprise.
'I've got to fetch my case,' says Laura.
'Dad will be here soon.'
She gets ready and waits.

The door bell rings. It must be Dad.
'Well, bye,' says Laura. 'I'm off.'
'Hey,' says Mum. 'Give me a kiss first.
And say goodbye to John properly.'
'Goodbye,' says John. 'I'm glad I met you.'
'Goodbye,' says Laura.
She stops for a minute, then says, 'See you soon.'
And she really hopes she will.

'You're very quiet,' says Dad.
'You're not ill, are you?'
Laura mumbles something. Should she tell him?
That John had sat at his place?
Will Dad be angry? Or sad?
Laura plucks up courage.
'Mum had a visitor.
A man, and he stayed for dinner.'

Dad just smiles and carries on driving.
'Don't you mind?' asks Laura.
'Mind? No, not at all. In fact, I think it's very good
for Mum, and for you and Thomas. Is he nice?'
Laura hesitates. 'Well, err, I think...'
She tries to find the right words.
'Yes,' she says at last. 'I like him.
But you will always be my dad.'